Emmanuel Guibert
Marc Boutavant
ARIOL
Bizzbilla Hits the Bullseye
PAPERCUTZ™

Bizzbilla Hits the Bullseye

*To Mister Guénier,*
*– Emmanuel Guibert*

# ARiOL

## #5 Bizzbilla Hits the Bullseye

Emmanuel Guibert – Writer
Marc Boutavant – Artist
Rémi Chaurand – Colorist
Joe Johnson – Translation
Bryan Senka – Lettering
Beth Scorzato – Production Coordinator
Michael Petranek – Associate Editor
Jim Salicrup
Editor-in-Chief



ISBN: 978-1-59707-735-4

Printed in China
August 2014 by New Era Printing, LTD.
Unit C. 8/F Worldwide Centre
123 Chung Tau, Kowloon
Hong Kong

Papercutz books may be purchased for business or promotional use. For information on bulk purchases please contact Macmillan Corporate and Premium Sales Department at (800) 221-7945 x5442.

Distributed by Macmillan
First Papercutz Printing

ARiOL
It's All Good
Well? What flavors?
Caramel chocolate!
Chocolate coconut for me!

It's good, eh?
Yeah, but you gotta lick fast 'cause it's running everywhere.
SLURP SLURP
SLURP SLURP
Where are we going, grandpa?
To the port to say hello to JUGGLE.
SLURP LAP
Look at the boats, RAMONO!
There's lots of seagulls!
SKREE
SKREE
SKRAW
SKREE
SKRAW

When it's low tide, the boats are way down at bottom of the quay.
How do you get down?

PLOOF
HEY, NOW!

HUMPH!
HAHA! Did you see that guy? He got a big glop of bird poop on his hat!

That's not bird poop, doofus! That's your ice cream!
Oh, yikes! Dang!
HEY, YOU KIDS!
Let's get out of here!
Okay.
Will you ask your grandpa to buy me another cone?
No. You should've paid attention.
But you're the one who told me to lean over!
Gimme some of yours.
Not too much, eh?
Are you coming, kids?

HELLO, JUGGLE!
HI, HOOFER! How's it chirping?
IT'S ALL GOOD

Still painting?
Yes. I'm touching it up.

Do you remember ARIOL, my grandson? He came with a buddy this year.
Wolf cub! Growing like weeds!

I'll give you my wrist, eh? I have paint all over my fingers.
Hello, Mister JUGGLE.
Hello, sir.
Can we go in your boat?
As much as you like.
Finish your ice cream first, you scamps!
They'll get chocolate stuck all over everything.
Bah! I'm repainting the hull. No worries up there.
Hey, RAMONO! You're a pirate. I'm THUNDER HORSE, and we're attacking Emperor MORODAN's ship!
Wait, I'm finishing my cone.
CRIITCH
CROUNTCH

PREPARE TO BOARD!
♫ Tonight, we'll set your plaaace-- Tonight, we'll set your place on fiiiire! ♫
There are guards, but I throw them in the water! POW! SPLASH!
And the sharks eat 'em!
It's too bad we're not on the real water.
We don't care, we act like we are. GIVE UP, MORODAN! TCHAK! TCHING!
While you're fighting with MORODAN, I'll steer the ship.
NO WAY! I'm steering!

I called it first!
Yes, but Mister JUGGLE is my grandpa's friend, so I'll steer first.
Let go of that wheel!
You let it go!
LOOK OUT! WE'RE HEADING TOWARDS THE ROCKS!
Whatever!
Are your two youngsters good kids?
A little lively, but they're fine.

HEY, gentlemen!
?
?
I'm looking for two kids who pelted my hat with ice cream from the quay five minutes ago. You haven't seen them, by any chance?
Uh, no.
That's not us, in any case.
It'll take me time, but I'll find them!
And then the blood will flow!
♫ You can't catch me-uh! Nanananananana-uh! ♫
You'll see!

Take that!
You're dumb! You threw Mister JUGGLE's brush into the sea!
It's no big deal, it's just a fake sea. We'll go look for it soon.
IT'S ALL GOOD
End

ARIOL
The Big Hug
A hug!
Mama's working, little foal.
CLIK CLIK
CLIK CLIK

Just a little one!
I have to finish this letter. It's super urgent.
CLIK
CLIK CLIK
CLIK

Come on, mommiepoo. One itty-bitty, wittle hug! All sweet and nice.
Wait a minute, ARIOL. Granny Annie's coming for dinner, I absolutely must get this done.
CLIK
CLIK
CLIK
CLIK

I love you, Mommy, dear.
And I adore you.
Then give me a hug.
CLIK
CLIK
CLIK

"Thank-you-for-your-kind-consideration. Sincerely-yours--"
PFooooo!
It's not fair!
CLIK
CLIK
CLIK

If that's how it is, I'm pouting.
Signed: MUE-SLI OA-TS.
There. Sent!
CLIK
SCHOOOOO!
So! Where's that poor, neglected little donkey?
Here.
Where's Mama's wittle baby foal? He's his Mama's wittle foal, he is.
The cuddle up! I want to do the cuddle up!
Isn't life nice, RIRI?
Yes.

Goodness, your ear is only sort of clean. Show me the other one.
No way! We're doing a hug, not getting cleaned up!
You'll wash all that for me before bed, eh?
Yes, yes.
And you'll clip your nails, too. Both hands and feet.
YES!
HEEHAWHEEHAWHEEHAW
Telephone. Excuse me.
Say we're not here.
Hello? Hi, SYNOVIA! Just fine, and you?
Darn. Mrs. STERN again.

I'll warn you we can't talk long because my mother's coming for dinner and nothing's ready--
With Mrs. STERN, phone calls always last an hour...
CLIK
CLAK
AH? Dad's home!
DADDY!
Good evening, son.
DADDY! DADDY! DADDY!
Waaait just one second. Let me put my stuff down.

Hi, Dad.
SMOOCH
Hi, kid.
SMACK
You doing all right?
I want a hug.
A hug? Good idea. We'll give each other a big hug, but first I'll go say hello to your mom.
Mom's on the phone with Mrs. STERN.
Oooooh, well then! I've got tons of time to wash my hands.
Was it a good day? Did you finish your homework?
Yes. I want a hug.

I'll just have a drink. My throat's dry. Are you thirsty?
No.
AAH! That does me good. While I'm at it, I'll nibble on a little cheese.
You want some?
No. I want a hug.
Okay, come with me. We'll sit peacefully in the living room with my little drink and have that much talked about hug.
I'll turn on the radio. That way, we'll listen to the seven o'clock news at the same time, eh?
CLICK
...Bla bla...

...Bla bla...
Sit on my lap.

...Bla bla...
Ewww! You smell of cheese!
Of course.

DING DONG!
Well, now! Who's ringing the doorbell?
...Bla bla...
I KNOW!

GRANNY ANNIE!
My sweetie pie!

Hello, Granny. I'd completely forgotten you were coming tonight.
Hello, Otis. Is my daughter here?
She's on the phone.
Did you bring me a surprise, Granny?
YEEEAAAHH! SWEEET! THUNDER HORSE's convertible! I didn't have it! I wanted it!
ARIOL, I didn't hear you say "thanks."
THANKS, GRANNY!
Are you happy, honey?
RIPP
TEAR

You spoil that kid too much.
BAH! He's my sweetie pie.
SHRED
Come give your Granny a hug, darling.
Bla bla
RRROOOAAARR
Eh, honey? Come give me a big hug.
Bla bla
Wait, Granny. I'm busy!
End

ARiOL
After the Rain Comes Fair Weather
Do you see the sky?
All dark gray.
It's going to rain! We've got to get inside!

I felt a drop! A big one!
Baaa! We're going to get wet!
That's it! It's raining!
Darn!
WAIT UP! BAAAA!
What's PHARMAFLUFF saying?
I don't know. Run!

Hey, guys! I'm taking cover!
BONNGG
?
?
You're crazy, ARIOL! Why'd you run into that big pole?
I didn't see it.
He's got rain all over his glasses.
It's dry here.
We lost PHARMAFLUFF and BATTLEMESS.
Baaa!
Ah, no! There's PHARMAFLUFF.

→BAA!←
I'm soaked!
→Baaa! Baaa!←
Poor little lamb!
Forget it. He doesn't hear.
Too bad for him.
BATTLEMESS is asleep even when he's walking.

Isn't that BATTLEMESS over there?
Yes.
HEY, BATTLEMESS! WE'RE HERE!

Okay, what do we do?
We wait for the rain to stop.
→Baaa!←
I don't want to wait here! I'll catch a cold!

PHARMAFLUFF-THE-SCAREDY-MUFF, if you don't wanna stay here, get out!
BAAA! D-DON'T P-PUSH!
HEY, listen. KWAX is playing his flute!
Will you loan me your flute?
I play this with my beak. You need an instrument for your snout.
Since that's how it is, I'll play the drums!
POOM TAC POOM TAC TAGADAGADA BOOM PSCHEEE RRATATATA BANG BANG!

And I'll sing: "THUNDER HORSE, AVENGER OF THE STARS!"
TATA POOM
TATA POOM
And I'll dance, look:
LALAEELALALAEELALAAA
ploom
ploom
⇒BAAA!⇐
THE WATER'S RISING! It's going to flood and we won't be able to le-e-eave!
Show us!
Oh, yeah, it's true! There's a big puddle all the way round. We're on an island!
Cool! We'll have to jump over the sea!
⇒BAA!⇐
I won't ever ma-a-ake it!

Hey, guys! Look! BATTLEMESS has found us!
Well? Why did you all start running like idiots?
Because of the rain, silly! You didn't notice it's raining?
Yes. A little.
But it's done now.
Are you kidding?
No. He's right.
It's done raining.

How did you get through the big puddle of water?
Well, like this. Watch.
SHOOSH
SHOOSH
SHOOSH
HAHAHA! He's walking right through it!
BATTLEMESS! COME BACK! I HAVE AN IDEA!
Do you mind carrying me on your back over the puddle?
No way. My backpack's heavy enough.
I'll carry it, if you like.

Okay then.
Give it here.
And there! Hi-oh, BATTLEMESS!
Settle down. There's no hurry.
SHOOSH
SHOOSH
SHOOSH
Those two are dumb!
Hey, KWAX! You coming? We're having a jump over the puddle contest!
Go ahead without me. I want to play my recorder some more.
Okay. Jump then.
See ya.

HUP!
I won!
No, me!
SHOOSH
SHOOSH
My shoes are full of water.
Me, too. Did you see the sky? It's all clear.
End

ARiOL
Riddles
Play a game?
We could ask each other riddles.
I'm driving. I'm not playing.

I have one: what's red, slobbers, and crawls on the ground?
I know. It's--
TUT TUT! You said you weren't playing.
ARIOL? Can you guess?
An alien?
No.
A monster?
No.
WHOA!
Hey! Look out!
SON OF A--! I think we have a flat!
Pull to the side.
A crab?

Yes, that's it. The tire's flat. Of all the luck!
Eh, Mom? A crab?
Wait, ARIOL. We're not playing now.

Get out of the car. I'm going to push it farther from the road.
I'll help you!

MUESLI, you take the wheel and steer us.
Gnnn... It's heavy!

It's heavy, but I'm THUNDER HORSE and I'm pushing with all my might! ->GNNeeeeee!<-
HEY! IT'S MOVING!
♫ THUNDER HOOORSE, AVENGER OF THE STAAAARS ♫
That's good. That'll do.
Just a little more, Dad. I love pushing!

Hey, Mom! I pushed the car with Dad, but I'm the one who made it move.
Good job, little foal.
I'm strong, eh?
Dad, what are you doing now?
We have to change the tire.
You wouldn't rather call roadside assistance?
We're not going to call roadside assistance to change a tire! Roadside service costs a fortune!
I'll change the tire for you.
ARIOL, let go of that wheel. You'll get dirty!
But I'm just taking off the tire!

Daddy'll take care of it. Don't touch anything. Before removing the wheel, we have to raise the car.
Raise the car?
Let's take out the baggage, so I can reach the spare and all the stuff.
THUNDER HORSE is going to lift the car.
HEHEH! They'll be surprised! One... two...
...three!
MMMPPFFF!

That's not the right grip. Facing the other way will be better. HEAVE--
HOOO...!
ARIOL, get away from there. And stop rubbing up against the car. It's disgusting!
OOOH! Just when I was going to lift it!
Now look! You're got crud all over you.
But it's to help Dad!
If you want to help me, don't touch anything.

How will you lift the car without me?
With the jack.
What's a "JAK"?
This.
And how does it work?
ARIOL, go play by yourself without getting close to the road. We'll call you when it's done.
But I'm interested in seeing how Daddy changes the tire.
Then let him do it and watch without talking.
The problem is that it's getting dark and I can't see too well. Look and see if the flashlight's in the glove box, MUESLI.
I'll go!

Which one is the glove box?
You don't want to grab your Twiddler and play quietly?
No.
I found the flashlight.
Go ahead, shine it on me.
Can I shine it, Mom?
What a mess! My pant legs are all filthy!
There's still time to call roadside assistance.
Hand me the flashlight, Mom.
ARIOL, THAT'S ENOUGH NOW! I'm doing something hard, now's not the time to make me mad!
Okay, okay...

Anyhow, I figured out the riddle.
What riddle?
The one about what's all red, slobbering, and crawling on the ground.
?
It's Daddy.
HAHAHAHA!
Stop moving that flashlight! I can't see anything!
End

ARiOL
In the CUCUFE Forest
Hello, Mrs. OATS?
Yes, this is she.
Hello. This is RAMONO's father.
Ah! Hello. How are you doing?
Well, thanks. And you, with this nice weather?
Doing just fine.
Am I disturbing you?
No, no, not at all. What's going on?
BEEP
BEEP
TOOT
PWAT

RAMONO is beside me here, and we're getting ready to go on a family picnic and gather some mushrooms in the CUCUFE forest. Would ARIOL like to come with us?
Pass me ARIOL, Dad!
ARIOL's right beside me, too. I'll pass him to you, he'll tell you.
Who is it?
PWEET TIC TAP
ARIOL? It's me.
Me who?
RAMONO. Me, my dad, DIDI and LAHURE are going mushroom-picking. You coming?
Wait, I'll ask my mom.
Can I, Mom?
Yes, but there are good mushrooms and bad mushrooms. You listen closely to RAMONO's dad, eh? He's the specialist.
Okay.
Super cool.

LATER, IN THE CUCUFE FOREST...
Who wants another hard-boiled egg?
Come on, ARIOL, let's go play soccer.
RAMO, finish eating first!
AMO, inis seating!
→Raaah!← I'm tired of sitting! It's too long!
DIDI, cut them a slice of cake so they can go play.
Inis seating!
ARIOL, thank your mama for her lovely marbled cake.
Yes, but she's not the one who made it.

Is that lady a sow?
What lady?
Your dad's wife.
Oh, DIDI!
No, DIDI isn't a sow, she's a BOAR.
A what?
A female boar.
In fact, her first husband, before she was with my dad, was a boar.
You dropped your cake.
Aw, DANG! It's all smashed!
Go get some more.
Gimme ball!

Cake! Amo inis seating.
Yes, cake. But don't touch it, it fell. It's gross.
YAHU inis seating.
Uh-- leave it. It's dirty, I tell you!
He's eating the cake off the ground.
Come play soccer.
Is he your little brother?
No, LAHURE is the son of DIDI and the boar. But he's like my little brother.

Don't boars usually have two big teeth that come out of their mouth?
Yes. LAHURE's a baby. They'll grow out later.
And DIDI? She doesn't have two big teeth?
Luckily not. Otherwise my dad couldn't kiss her on the mouth.
HAHA!
A BIT LATER...
LET'S GO A-PICKING!
ETSOAICKING!
You put the ball in your mushroom pail?
YES. That way, if we get bored looking for mushrooms, we can play soccer.

ARIOL, we're going to teach you something important today: to recognize the smell of mushrooms. Aren't we, RAMONO?
Yep.
But ARIOL doesn't have a snout like us, so maybe he'll have more trouble getting the smells.
No, no, no. He'll do just fine, you'll see.
So, first we stop, open wide our nostrils, and take a deep breath.
SNNF!
SNFF?
SNF!
SNF?
And next, you catch a strong, slightly rancid smell: the mushroom's odor. You smell it?
No.
SNF!
No.

Do you smell it, DIDI?
Kinda.
SNF?
SNF?
But it's pretty distinct! An odor that you recognize!
SNF?
SNFF?
Search. They mustn't be far. Look under the ferns.
SNF SNF SNF
Can't see anything.
SNF?
That's it! I smell something, too!
SNF!
Ah! You see, RAMONO? Your buddy ARIOL has a better nose than you!
I smell that LAHURE has pottied in his diaper.
WHAT?

Let's see?
AYAHU POOPOOED DIAPA!
SNF SNF SNF
HAHAHAHA! That was my mushroom smell!
HAHAHA! HEEHEE!
MUSHROO!
HAHA!
Do you have a spare diaper, DIDI?
Always. Come on, baby boar. Mama's going to clean your bottom.
Mushroo AYAHU.
Catch, ARIOL!
Too hard!
BOP

HEY! COME LOOK!
What did you find?
Some mushrooms.
And good ones, too! Parasol mushrooms! Good job, ARIOL!
ARIOL's not the one who found them. My ball did!
End

ARIOL
ARIOL Defends Santa Claus
Are we going to the toy department, Granny? That way, you can buy my Christmas present.
Later, Sunshine. First, Granny has to return her coffeemaker.
RGOTS
99
RALINES

What's wrong with your coffeemaker?
It makes bad coffee. Before, I had an old machine that made extra good coffee, but it died.
Buy the same kind.
You can't find that model anymore.
Come up to the toy department then.
Hello, sir. I'm here to return this coffee machine.
Granny?
Do you have your receipt?
My receipt? Uh... yes. It must be in my change purse.
Granny!
We don't exchange any-thing without a receipt.

I can go to the toy department by myself. And you can join me.
That's strange, I was sure I grabbed it...
Nét
⇒PFFFF!⇐ I'm bored!
BHL
What's Santa Claus doing there?
VHS - DVD -
MP3 - DIVX
VHS - DVD -
Hello, young foal. Do you want a flyer? There's a contest.
What do you win? Games?
No.

You win living room furniture.
I don't care about living room furniture.
Me neither.
Yes, but I'm stuck here.
Well, me, too.

Why aren't you in the toy department then? That's where the kids go.
Santa Clauses, too, usually.

You know what? You make me want to take a break. You want some orange juice?
No thanks. On the other hand, I'd like to try on your beard.

HAHA! Nice! If RAMONO could see me now!
Put the hat on, too.
Who's RAMONO?
He's my best friend. A piglet. He's so nice.
And what's your name?
ARIOL. You know, I stuck up for you at school once?
How's that?
It's when I was in the last year of pre-school. There was a guy in my class whose name was TARTELON. One day, he said to me: "Santa Claus ain't real!"
Oh!

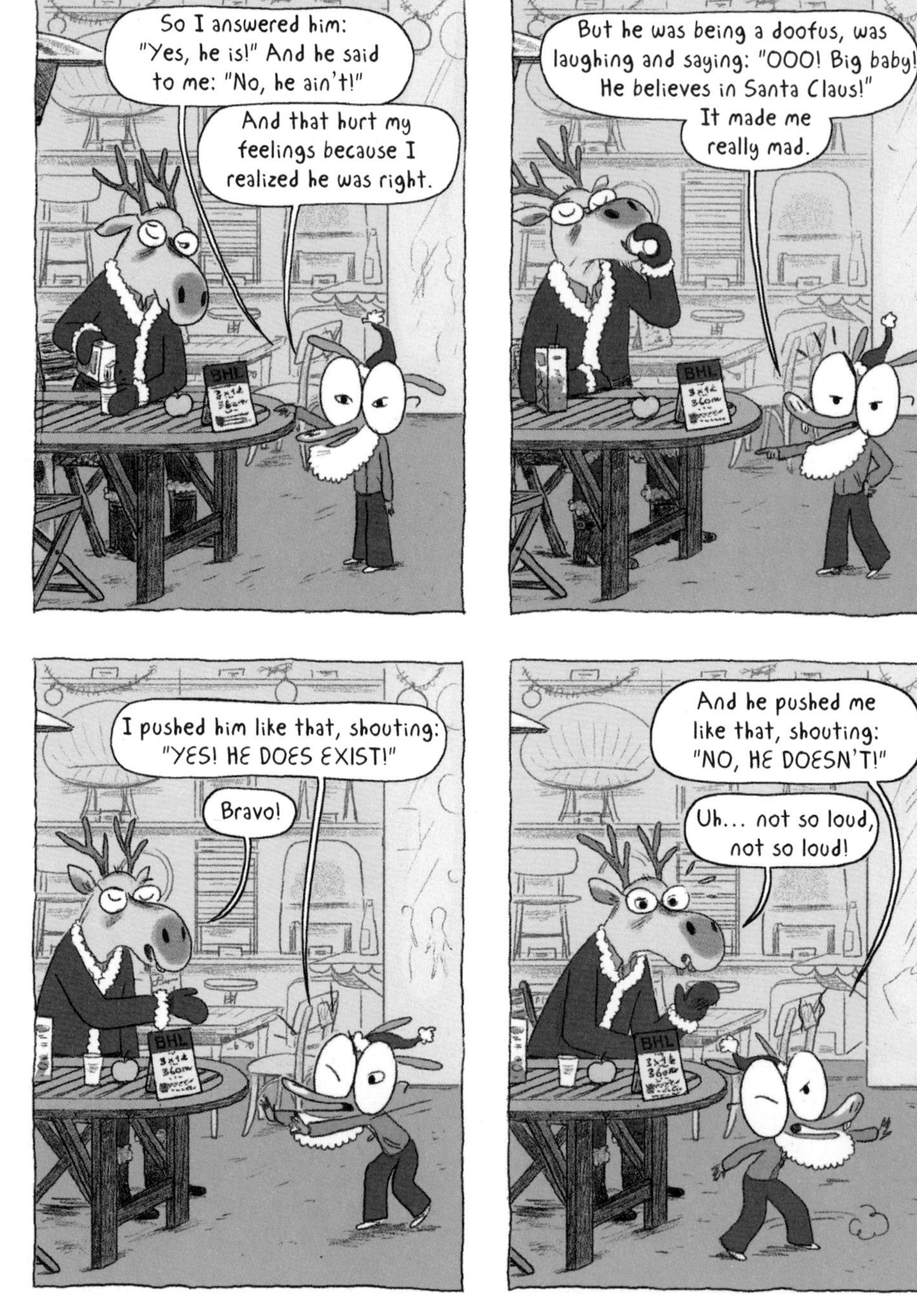
So I answered him: "Yes, he is!" And he said to me: "No, he ain't!"
And that hurt my feelings because I realized he was right.
But he was being a doofus, was laughing and saying: "OOO! Big baby! He believes in Santa Claus!"
It made me really mad.
I pushed him like that, shouting: "YES! HE DOES EXIST!"
Bravo!
And he pushed me like that, shouting: "NO, HE DOESN'T!"
Uh... not so loud, not so loud!

So I pushed him back harder--
Well now, Santa Claus!
We're not paying you to have a drink with the kids, eh? You have flyers to hand out.
I'm entitled to a break, though!
Back to work! Get a move on!
There's no point coming in tomorrow. I'll replace you.
But...
Hey, sir!
In fact, Santa Claus was explaining to me what you do to get living room furniture. And it's super interesting.
Oh, yeah?

Yes. I'm going to tell my granny to come buy some. And my daddy and mommy, too. And my friends.
Why that's perfect.
You're a very nice, little foal. Would you like to keep Santa Claus' beard and cap?
Oh, yes!
They're yours.
You go look for others in back. And I take back what I said: I'll keep you. Tomorrow, you'll go to the toy department.
Good.
Buddy, you're a true defender of Santa Clauses. In the name of all Santa Clauses, I thank you.
It's nothing.

ARIOL, where were you? I've been looking for you for ten minutes.
I was with Santa Claus, Granny. Look, he gave me his beard and his hat!
Come, now. I can't find my receipt, and they're refusing to exchange my coffee maker.
Will we go to the toy department then?
Excuse me, ma'am, but what kind of coffee maker are you looking for?
An old model that no longer exists, alas! A MOOLUX.
Wait for me here.
A bit later...
You found another beard and cap?
Yes, and that's not all.

Here!
OOOOOH! My old MOOLUX!
Brand new!
You're-- you're--
Santa Claus, ma'am.
Okay. Can we go to the toys now?
Come back and see me. Starting tomorrow, I'll be in the toy department, too. I'll get you some little presents. And bring that buddy of yours--
RAMONO!
TOYS
End

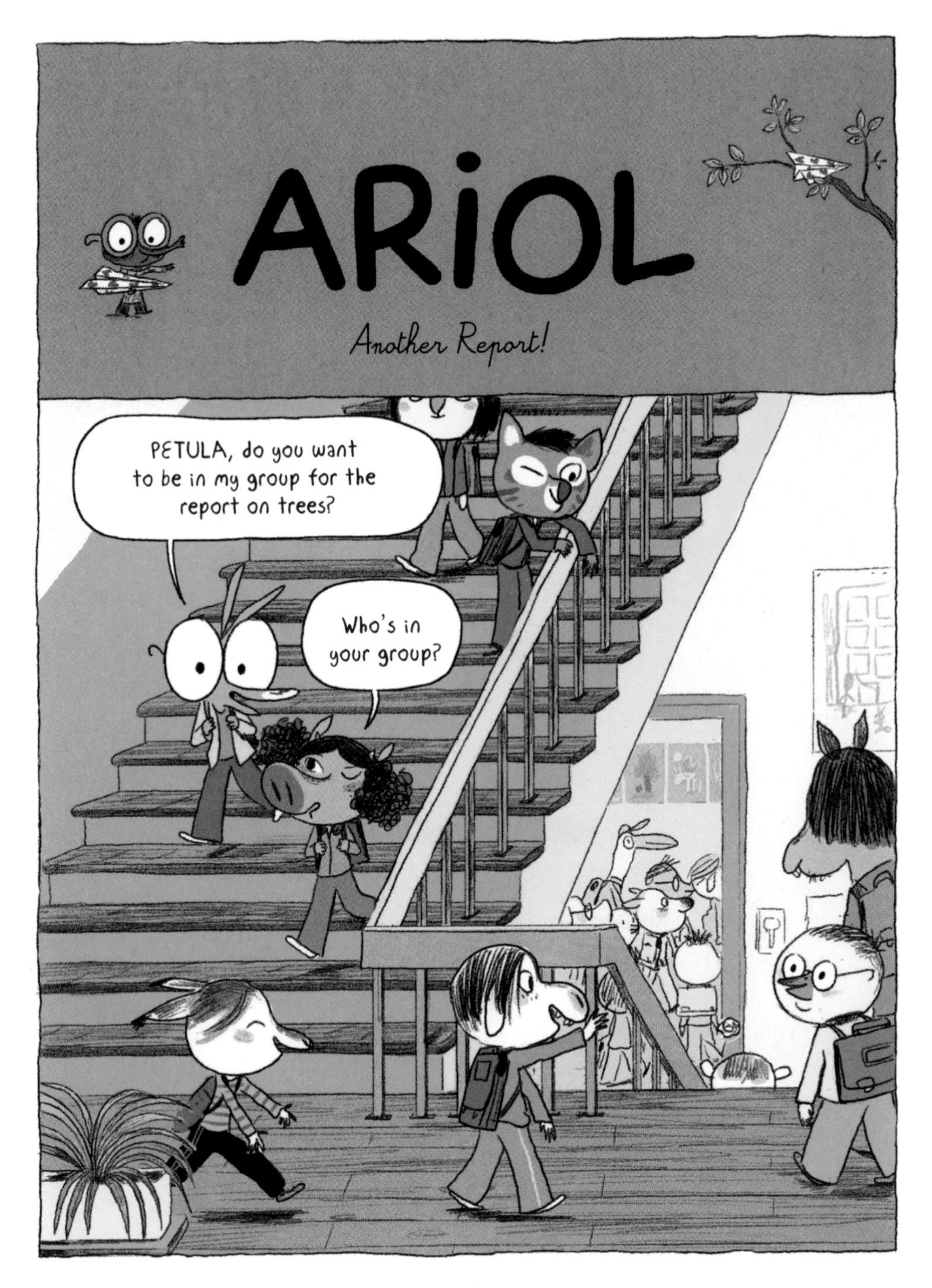
ARiOL
Another Report!
PETULA, do you want to be in my group for the report on trees?
Who's in your group?

Well, there's me and RAMONO.
No, thank you! RAMONO's useless. Anyways, I'm already doing a report on glaciers with MOTHBELLA and SHABILLY.
-Sigh-
Hey, ARIOL!
Good news! BIZZBILLA wants to do the report with us.
?
It seems you asked for me, ARIOL? Here I am!
TIMBERWOLF and BOUNCER wanted me to go with them, but I said "no." They just want me because I'm the best in class, to get a good grade without working.
They're dummies.

We want you because we're friends. Right, ARIOL?
Yes, I know ARIOL's nice.
You, RAMONO, on the other hand, always make fun of me.
BAH, not to be mean. Just for laughs.
It doesn't make me laugh.
If you want, ARIOL, we can go to the library tomorrow afternoon. We'll do research on the computer and look at books.
Cool!
We're gonna get a good gra-ade, We're gonna get a good gra-ade!
Shut up, you annoy me!

THE NEXT DAY, AT THE LIBRARY...
Hi, BIZZBILLA.
Hello, ARIOL. You did well to come without RAMONO. We'll work better.

PEEKABOO! Guess who?
?

Idiot! You've put fingerprints on my glasses!
That hurts less than a finger in your eye!

This computer here is free. ARIOL, sit down beside me and take notes.
And what do I do?
You're going to look in the books over there to see if you find something.
No way! I prefer the computer.
ARIOL's the one who'll look in the books!
ARIOL is staying with me!
Ooooh! No!

How come I'm not preparing a report on glaciers with PETULA? Why is life so unfair?
LET US WORK, RAMONO!
Oh, okay. All right...

That pig is clingy!
Sometimes, yes.
You know, ARIOL, I already looked at home on the INTERBEAST for things on trees. I can explain everything to you.
Great.
But it'd be best to leave here.
Really?
Yes. Because the trees are outside.
And it's springtime outside. So the trees are budding. That means the leaves are starting to come out. And it's pretty to look at.
Oh, yeah?
Come, let's go.

But uh... And Ramono?
ARIOL!
We don't care about RAMONO!
Look what I found!
WHOOOA!
The THUNDER HORSE ENCYCLOPEDIA! WHERE'D YOU GET IT?
From over there. This library is too cool!
BIZZBILLA, you can continue the report in peace. We won't bother you anymore.
HOHO! Look, RAMONO: A portrait of THUNDER HORSE when he was little!

And here's the baby Emperor MORODAN!
HAHAHA! He's so ugly! He looks like BIZZB--
Where'd she go?
I don't know!

BIZZBILLA?

BIZZBILLA?
BIZZBIIIILLA?

HEY! Quiet, children! You're in a library, not in your playground.
But it's because we lost a friend!
A little fly with big glasses.
I just saw her leave. She didn't look happy, either. You weren't mean to her?
Oh, no, no!
On the contrary, we adore her.
She's got nerve taking off like that without saying anything. Who'll do the report now?
Come on, we'll catch her.
BIZZBIIIIIIIILLA!
WHERE ARE YOU?

Maybe she's hiding.
No, I don't think so. She must have gone home.
Dang!
Look, we don't need her to say what a tree's like. It's tall, with a brown trunk, with roots at the bottom, with branches up high, and green leaves stuck on it.
You're right.
ARY
Want to go back in the library to look at THE THUNDER HORSE ENCYCLOPEDIA?
Oh, yes! For once, I love a book!
End

ARIOL
RIKA
Come look, ARIOL. You have a visitor.
Who is it? RAMONO?
Thunder Horse
in WINTER
VH
THU
HOR

Look who's here.
?
Ooooooh! I don't believe it!

This big boy is ARIOL?
Oh, yes.
It's not possible! A real gentleman!

And me? Do you recognize me?
Uh...
You don't recognize me!

You boys are all the same! They forget fast! HeeHeeHee!
This is RIKA, ARIOL. She was your babysitter when you were very little.
Well, then? You won't give your little RIKA a kiss?
Uh... yes.
SMACK
SMACK
My little foal! You're the cutest!
We sure did lots of things together, you know! I gave you your bottle, washed your butt, pushed you in your walker... At first, you were hardly this big.

And TANGO MILONGA? Do you remember when we'd dance TANGO MILONGA?
No.
Give me your hands.
Now, step on my feet.
I won't hurt you, miss?
Call me RIKA, silly.
♫ There, like that. And we'd turn, while singing: TANGO MILONGA ♫
HEY!
TANGO MER'H MAJEGN ICHNOUFF!
This deserves a photo.

HeeHeeHee! You loved that! You'd laugh like crazy! We had to start over right up again!
Look at me, both of you.
What can I get for you, RIKA? You want some tea? Coffee? Fruit juice?
Tea would be nice. Thanks.
Will you show me your room? I want to see if it has changed.
Yes.
Beautiful room! Goodness, you've put up lots of posters!
It's THUNDER HORSE.

Ah yes, I remember! You already had a THUNDER HORSE blankie when you were a baby.
THUNDER HORSE is stronger than everything.
You'd say to me: "RIKA, I WAN YOUR ZEEK!" And you'd rub my cheek with your hand. Then, you'd sniff it. It was to smell my perfume.
And I have his glowing horseshoe, too.

I have his magic lasso and I have a Twiddler with lots of games. And I have all the DVDs.
You know what you'd do when you were three?

Here, have a little cheek.

Breathe.
SNIFF?
Who babysits you now when your dad and mom aren't home?
Mrs. CAPRA. She's the neighbor on the third floor.

Well?
It smells good.
I liked it when you'd do that.

Is she nice?
Yes, but she's old and she makes creamed carrots too much.
HeeHeeHee!

Later...
Thanks for the tea. It made me really happy to see you both again.
Us, too. Come back whenever you like.
Hey. RIKA!
What do you want, little foal?
Will you give me a little more cheek?
Go ahead. Have two of them.
Will you come babysit me sometimes?
Ah, babysit you, no. I don't have time now, I work. But I'll come back and see you, I promise.

When you leave the building, look up. I'll wave to you from the balcony.
Okay.
These photos of you and RIKA dancing TANGO MILONGA are good.
Show me.

SNIFF!
Will you print them?
If you want. I'll send them to RIKA, too. She gave me her eBEAST address.

Come on, let's wave to her from the balcony.
Good idea.
Seeing old friends again is nice, eh?
Really nice.
GOODBYE, RIKA!
BYE BYE, OATS! See you around!
End

ARiOL
The Tattooed Ear
What can I get for you, sweeties?
We want two mint BUBBLES!
The ones with the THUNDER HORSE tattoos.
BREAD

What's the password?
Please, Mrs. POMPADOUR.
That's better.
And the other password?
Thanks, Mrs. POMPADOUR!
Ah! There you go!

There. That'll be fifty cents.
I'm opening mine.
BREAD
You can't. Wait for me!

People think my job is being a baker but, no! I educate children!
Absolutely. Parents nowadays don't say anything to them. Back when I was little--
BREAD

Let me see. What's your tattoo?
And what's yours?
Mine's better.
That's right. Mine is, too.
Where do we stick them?
We have to choose the right place.
What if you put it under your ear?
You're crazy! Under an ear is no good. Nobody would see it.

Well, no, just the opposite, it's funny. You come up to someone and say: "Did you see what I have in my ear?" And HUP! You lift it!
And the other person is surprised.
You do it.
I can't. My ears stick up in the air. It'd be too obvious. Yours fall just right.
Okay. So, you'll help me?
Lean over.
Don't pull on it, eh? I don't want a donkey ear.
Don't move.
Wait a bit for it to stick.
My sister hasn't told my mom, but she got a real tattoo done. One that won't go away. A bird.

And do you know where she put it?
No.
On her back.
She can't even see it! My sister is stupid. What's more, her bird was done badly. It looks like a stain.
Don't move, I said.
Okay, I'm tired of this. Are you done?
Almost.
Theeere...
Lemme see?

We need a mirror.
Come on, let's cross the street. We'll look in the drugstore window.
Oh, yeah, that's not bad. I like it.
I told you so.
Where're you going?
Into the drugstore.
Do you want to buy something?
You'll see.

Nothing stupid, eh? This is the drugstore where my mom goes. They know me here.
Don't worry.

Hello, gentlemen.
Hello. This ear hurts.

Show it to me, boy.
Inside.

OOOH! I see!
HAHAHA! It's a joke!

Ah, no, it's not a joke! On the contrary, it's very serious.
Yes, it IS a joke. It's a THUNDER HORSE tattoo!
Look.
Ah, yes, I see. It's bizarre. Show me the other ear.
ARIOL! Tell them it's for a laugh!

MRS. BEPPER, come look. This little pig has an ear problem.
No, I don't have a problem!
ZIPZAP
ARIOL!
RAMONO's crazy. I'll act like I don't know him.

What's more, since
I don't know him,
I'll leave...
I'll look for some cotton and alcohol. We must disinfect it all.
That would be best.
Oh, no, no, no! I'm leaving! My mom's expecting me!
GOODBYE, EVERYBODY!
?
HAHAHA!
We still know how to play jokes, too!
Ah, children nowadays, I swear! Always running everywhere! Back when I was little...

Let's escape, QUICK!
You're crazy, RAMONO!
Why'd you abandon me?
I didn't abandon you. I went outside to put my tattoo on my shoulder.
Wow, they didn't get the joke.
You have to play jokes on friends. Adults never understand.
End

ARiOL
RAMONO and SPELLERINO
There's nothing on TV tonight. We're going to play a game of SPELLERINO.
SUPER! SPELLERINO!
Are you playing, HOOFER? It'll entertain the kids.
BAH, if you want. I rather read my newspaper.

Do you know this game, RAMONO?
No.
We'll explain it to you. You'll see, it's easy. ARIOL's very good at it.
With SPELLERINO, you learn lots of words, and how they're spelled also.
Granny always wins.
Not surprising! She spends an hour on each word!
Everyone has their little letter holder? We'll draw our letters. Seven per player.
Uh... I don't really like games with letters. I'll just watch you.
No, don't worry! Play with us.
All right, let's go. You start, ARIOL, and explain to your friend what you're doing.
Yes.
Not too fast, eh?

So, look: I have my seven letters on the holder and I have to make a word out of them.
Pfff! It's like school!
For example, here, I can write BOOTS: B, two Os, T, S.
What's that?
Well, boots. Like THUNDER HORSE wears boots.
Oh, yeah.
Or rain boots.
Since I'm the one starting, I'll put my letters in the middle.
Putting your boots on the table isn't polite.
HAHAHA!
Okay, that makes six points, but since ARIOL is starting, we multiply by two: two times six, twelve.
Oh, dang! You have to do math, too!
Don't worry, I tell you. Granny's the one who counts.

Grandpa's turn, now.
It's simple with me. I have one rule, I play fast. The faster you play, the faster we go to bed.
So, I use ARIOL's "S" and I write SLATE.
Not so good. Five points.
And since it's Annette's turn, I'll have time to go shut all the house's shutters.
I'll make a quick bathroom run.
Ah well, no, don't leave me! I'm coming with you.
TUT TUT! Stay, RAMONO. It's your turn after me.
But, ma'am, I don't understand anything! I can't write BOOTS, like ARIOL. I don't have the letters I need!
First, I've already told you that here, nobody calls me "ma'am." Just call me GRANNY ANNETTE.

Next, you mustn't write ARIOL's word. You must write your own, with your letters.
Yes, but I don't like to write very much, ma'am. I prefer watching TV or playing video games. Or even going to bed.
Watch my letters, you'll see. I had a good draw. I can write at least three different words.
OOOH... I'm tired of this... I wanna leave.
I have to choose the one that'll bring me the most points. And for that, I have to think. Thinking is fun. Do you want to help me?
Uh... yes. But while you're thinking, I'll go have a drink in the kitchen. I'm real thirsty.
Come back fast, eh?
Yes, yes!

ARIOL? You there?
What do you want?
YOU'RE CRAZY! IT'S NIGHTTIME!

I can't take anymore SPELLERMAJIG. I'm leaving.
Huh? Where to?
I don't know. To the yard.

I gotta hide...
I'll say I went outside to pee in the yard because ARIOL was in the bathroom and that I got lost...
I'll get behind ARIOL's grandpa's oil tank.
There. Nobody'll find me here.
YAP! YAP! YAP!
Aw, darn! It's that stupid REX!

YAP! ARF ARF! YAP!
Down, REX! Go back inside!
What are you doing here, kid?
AAAH!
YAP! YAP!
You scared me.
I came back with REX to close the gate. Are you hiding?
No. Well, yes.
Sir, rescue me! I don't wanna play that letters game! It's too hard, I don't understand it at all.
HAHAHA! My goodness, you ran away to escape SPELLERINO!

I understand you, you know. SPELLERINO bores me stiff, too. But don't call me "sir," call me "Grandpa." It's more laid back.
RAMONO!
YAP!
Hey, why are you all outside?
Your buddy is allergic to SPELLERINO.
I swear to you, ARIOL, vacations at your grandpa and grandma's is really nice. But if I have to write complicated stuff every night, then I'd rather go back to my mom's.
Whoa there! Don't have a conniption!
We'll explain to Granny Annette that you don't want to play and that's it. She'll understand.
It's no use. Come look.

ANNETTE is so absorbed with her move she doesn't realize we're not there. We're safe for the moment.
What do we play then?
Nothing. We sit down and daydream. It's cool tonight, and the sky's pretty clear.
Yes, but we want to play something. We'll get bored otherwise.
We could play learning the names of stars.
Okay.
You're just making me mad! It's a vacation! I'm telling you I don't wanna learn anything at all!
End

ARIOL
Market Day at Saint-Ampoire
Hello, my dear. What can I get you?
Hello, YODETTE. Give me five fresh sardines, it's so we can have them raw.
Ah! Good idea!

Do you like fish, RAMONO?
Meh.
You'll see: raw sardines with a slice of lemon, bread, and butter are delicious. Isn't that true, ARIOL?
Yes.
Here, my dear. Look how pretty that is. They look like they're going to talk. Do I fix them for you?
No, thanks. I'll do them myself.
Hey, RAMONO! Did you hear what the seller called my granny?
No.
She called her "my dear." And she calls my grandpa "my dear." She calls everyone "my dear."
If you talk to her, she'll call you "my dear," too.
No way! She's too ugly! You talk to her.
Okay. Watch.

Mrs. YODETTE?
Yes? What does that little dear want?
What's wrong with that, little dear?
ARIOL, stop acting foolish!
It's-- it's cold down my back!

AAAH!
?
?

An ice cube!
HAHA HAHA!

Did you do that to me, you idiot?
No, my dear.
Those little dears look like they're having fun. How long will you have them?
Three weeks.
Should I include a few periwinkles with that?
No, thanks, that'll do.
Hello, my dear. What can I get you?
Let's go to the creamery now. And be good.
You're stupid with your ice cube. Don't ever do that again.
AAAH! It's cooold down my baaack!
HAHA!

Are things going as you like, Mrs. OATS?
They're fine, Mr. QUATREMEC. Give me twelve extra-large eggs and my husband's camembert.
Well-aged, like usual.
Are you still not eating cheese, ARIOL?
I'll eat it if there's no smell and there's no taste. But I prefer yogurt.
And you, pet?
My mom buys MUHMUH. It's a spread. Sometimes, there are stickers in the box. My sister eats the MUHMUH, and I put up the stickers.
It's time to make these children discover real cheese. Here, taste that, I'm sure you'll like it.
What is it?
I'll tell you afterwards.

It's weird. It's all orange.
It smells a little.
Eat, you silly geese! Since Mr. QUATREMEC's giving it to you!
Well?
I don't really like it. It has a taste.
ARH! Hard to please!
I like it.
There's one fan at least! It's called MIMOLETTE. Pretty name, eh?
It's good.
Can I have more?
You say: "please, Mr. QUATREMEC."
HAHA! I teach them about cheese and you teach them politeness. We've got some work!

Here, kid, enjoy yourself.
Since he likes that, put in a small slice for me.
Thanks, sir.
?
YEEOOWWW!
?
YOU'RE CRAZY! YOU HURT ME!
Not me, my dear.
Sir, he pricked my butt with your toothpick, and my piece of mimolettuce fell on the ground!
And just a bit ago, he put one of Mrs. YODETTE's ice cubes in my tee-shirt.
THAT'S ENOUGH!

Instead of bickering, you'll make yourselves useful. ARIOL, you'll carry the cheese, and RAMONO will carry the fish. I'll keep the eggs. That's safer.
I was going to advise that.
Come on! Let's get the fruit and veggies. Goodbye and thanks, Mister QUATREMEC.
Have a good day, Mrs. OATS. See you next time, kids!
Yuck! My bag stinks. It's grandpa's camembert.
Wanna switch?
That one stinks of fish.
I'm gonna have a little piece of mimilettuce.

Oh! A car and a motorcycle that move if you put in money! You got any money?
No.

Ask your granny!
I'd be surprised if she gave me some, because we made her a little mad with our jokes. Granny ANNETTE is stricter than my other granny.
Well, too bad, we'll get in anyways. We'll pretend it's moving.
We can't. Granny will scold us, if we lose her.

She's over there. She sees us. Come on, climb on a sec.
Okay, but wait. Don't go without me.
Your motorcycle stinks of cheese.
And your car is full of rotten fish.
Can you imagine if we went home like this?
It'd be too cool.
End

ARiOL
Thanks, BIZZBILLA
You look funny, ARIOL. What's wrong? Are you feeling unwell?
I feel groggy.
That's the second time this week.
ERIKA NO

Show me your forehead. Do you feel feverish?
No.
COUTOS
I wonder if your glasses are matching your sight. We'll get an appointment with BIZZBILLA's father for a check-up.
When my glasses are clean, I see really well through them.
The next day, at school...
I have an appointment with your dad so he'll look at my eyes.
Oh, yes? When?
Saturday morning.
That's great! You'll come to my home!
Well, yes, I have to. I'd like to ask you for a favor...
Go on.

Every time I go see your dad, he takes off my glasses and makes me read letters on the wall.
He does that to everyone. It's to check your sight.
It annoys me.
At first, the letters are big and I can manage to read them. But afterwards, they get really tiny and I can't see anything.
That's because you're near-sighted, like me. It's no biggie.
I don't like it when I can't read any further. I'm ashamed.
You're crazy! You shouldn't be!
And your father scares me. He's strict.
No. He's not strict. He's just shy and has his head in the clouds a little.
Please, BIZZBILLA. Saturday morning, could you whisper the little letters to me?

Saturday morning...
Look, ARIOL. BIZZBILLA's waiting for us at the door.
Yoohoo!

Hello, BIZZBILLA. My goodness, you dressed up nice.
Hello, ma'am. Hello, ARIOL.
Hi, BIZZBILLA.

It's nice of you to welcome us like that.
Go into the waiting room. I made some orange juice and cookies for you.

Here, serve yourselves.
OOOH! Why that's adorable! You shouldn't have gone to such trouble.
CRUNCH
Is your daddy okay with us eating in the waiting room? Does he know?
Uh... yes, yes. No problem.
Gulp.

Don't get your crumbs everywhere, ARIOL.
I don't have crumbs.
It's okay. I'll sweep.

BIZZBILLA! WHAT ARE YOU UP TO?
Huh?

Who let you bring food in here? You know it's against the rules!
But, Daddy, I...
Hello, ma'am. Excuse the little--
Hello, Doctor CANTHARIDE >crunch<. Don't scold BIZZBILLA. She'sh welcoming us like a real princesh >crunch crunch<.
>Crunch.<
This is my friend ARIOL, Daddy. You know him, he's come before. He's in class with me.
Ah, yes, okay. Hello, ARIOL.
Hello, shir >crunch<.
This way, follow me. And you, BIZZBILLA, carry all of that back to the kitchen, please.
Yes, Daddy.

A bit later...
Let's start with the little letters. When you can no longer read them, you say: "I can't."
Well, darn! Where's BIZZBILLA? She promised she'd help me!
HFEP
TGNR
DMKX

This one?
HFEP
TGNR
TAP
TAP

Oh, no, I'm seeing all blurry. It's impossible to read...
An F? An X?
Bzzzt!

G
M

TOC TOC
A “G”!
Yes. Next letter.

An “M”!
Yes. Next letter.

At the end of the check-up...
ARIOL's doing very well. It's strange, but his sight has improved instead.
Now there's good news!
Thanks, BIZZBILLA. You were cool to do that.
You can come back when you like, eh? Even if you don't have an appointment with my father.
See you Monday at school!
Till Monday!
Your friend BIZZBILLA's really nice
That's true. Did you see how well I read?

In BIZZBILLA's bedroom...
SLURP.
The glass ARIOL drank out of...
CRUUNCH.
The cookie he bit into--
Thanks, BIZZBILLA You're cool.
A R I O L
MUNCH MUNCH
End

# WATCH OUT FOR PAPERCUTZ

Welcome to the fifth, fly-frustrating ARIOL graphic novel, by the exceptionally talented team of Emmanuel Guibert and Marc Boutavant, from Papercutz, those funny humans dedicated to publishing great graphic novels for all ages. I'm Jim Salicrup, Editor-in-Chief and one-time participant in a Raid TV commercial. I'd like to take a moment or two to share a few random ARIOL thoughts...

First off, ARIOL just got one of the cutest reviews ever! You can find it here: boingboing.net/2014/02/27/guest-review-my-daughter-revi.html. That six-year-old Poesy shows excellent taste. Her father, Cory Doctorow, usually has wonderful taste as well, but for reasons unknown, when it comes to ARIOL, he may have misjudged our favorite blue donkey. Fortunately, he respects his daughter's taste and lets her enjoy ARIOL-- both the graphic novels available from Papercutz and the YouTube videos of the animated series. Hey, Cory-- want to do a graphic novel for Papercutz about the coolest pain-free pediatrician in the world? We'll call it DOCTOR OW!

Maybe it's just me, but whenever I see the name "BIZZBILLA," I sing it to myself as "Bismillah" like in the classic Queen song "Bohemian Rhapsody."

Back in ARIOL #4, I showed you that great pic of me "kissing" Emmanuel Guibert via Skype at a Marc Boutavant appearance at Bergen Street Comics in Brooklyn. This time around I offer this pic of me with Marc at that same appearance...

Marc is truly an amazing artist, and it's great to just watch him draw! It's almost like watching a magician, but instead of pulling a rabbit (or a RABBID) out of his hat, Marc is able to bring the cast of ARIOL into our world. Now that's real magic!

That's enough ARIOL stuff for now. I've got to practice for the upcoming Spellerino championship before ARIOL #6 comes out. Until then, I hope you don't forget we're all just a donkey, like you and me!

Thanks,

Jim


## STAY IN TOUCH!

EMAIL: salicrup@papercutz.com
WEB: papercutz.com
TWITTER: @papercutzgn
FACEBOOK: PAPERCUTZGRAPHICNOVELS
REGULAR MAIL: Papercutz, 160 Broadway, Suite 700, East Wing, New York, NY 10038

# Other Great Titles From PAPERCUTZ™

And Don't Forget . . .
All-new, full-color Graphic Novel
Thea Stilton
THE TREASURE OF THE VIKING SHIP
PAPERCUTZ
ONE FULL-COLOR SMURFS STORY BY Peyo
THE FINANCE SMURF
PAPERCUTZ
GERONIMO STILTON © ATLANTYCA SPA ALL RIGHTS RESERVED
...available at your favorite booksellers.